THIS BOOK BELONGS TO

For Sandy, a bright shining star taken too soon - AW

For Emmy, I love you - CHH

Special thanks to Gussie, Paul, Jack and all Benny's wonderful fans - LDB

Published by Little Door Books 2020
This edition published 2020

ISBN: 978-1-9999655-5-6

Little Door Books

mail@littledoorbooks.co.uk
www.littledoorbooks.co.uk
twitter: @littledoorbooks

ONE BUTTON BENNY

AND THE
GIGANTIC CATASTROPHE

WRITTEN BY ALAN WINDRAM

ILLUSTRATED BY CHLOE HOLWILL-HUNTER

Benny was different. Benny was special. Benny was a ROBOT...

...who HATED washing the dishes!

He would try anything to get out of doing them.

IS THIS AN EMERGENCY? CAN I PRESS MY BUTTON?

NO BENNY... IT'S DEFINITELY NOT AN EMERGENCY! IT'S YOUR TURN!

CAN'T SPARKY DO THEM? SHE'S REALLY GOOD AT WASHING DISHES.

Sparky was Benny's cat.

As Benny tried sneaking away his mum shouted...

Benny had almost forgotten about Cool Cat.
Sparky loved getting polished up and made to look all shiny.

As he stood at the sink, Benny remembered all that had happened when there had been a real emergency and he had pressed his Big Bright Red Button.

What an adventure that had been.

Outside, Benny's friends were so excited about Cool Cat they were busy pampering their pets.

They would press their buttons and soap, polish and shining cloths would appear. Some of them even had special sparkling spray which made their cats look amazing.

Benny couldn't press his button because it wasn't an emergency, so he washed, then polished Sparky, and in the end she looked as sparkly and shiny as all the other cats.

The next morning when Benny and his friends woke up,
something terrible had happened.

All of their cats had vanished!

They hunted all over the town for their missing pets but they were nowhere to be seen. They had just disappeared.

The only thing that they found was
a mysterious note lying on the ground.

Benny ran to his mum and said

So Benny placed his finger over the big bright red button on his tummy,

closed his eyes, and pressed his button...

but nothing happened.

Then everyone heard a loud CLUNK and a CREAK as Benny's Button opened up like a door and two bits of paper dropped out.

CLUNK!

ONLY PRESS IN AN EMERGENCY

CREAK!

'That's weird,' thought Benny.
'This wasn't what happened the last time I pressed my button.
This must be what we need to save the cats.'

Looking at the paper,
Benny realised it was a plan.

On the paper were instructions on how to build a GIGANTIC cat out of scrap metal. The cat had a secret door in it so that Benny and his friends could hide inside.

So everybody worked together and soon they had built the biggest metal cat anyone had ever seen.

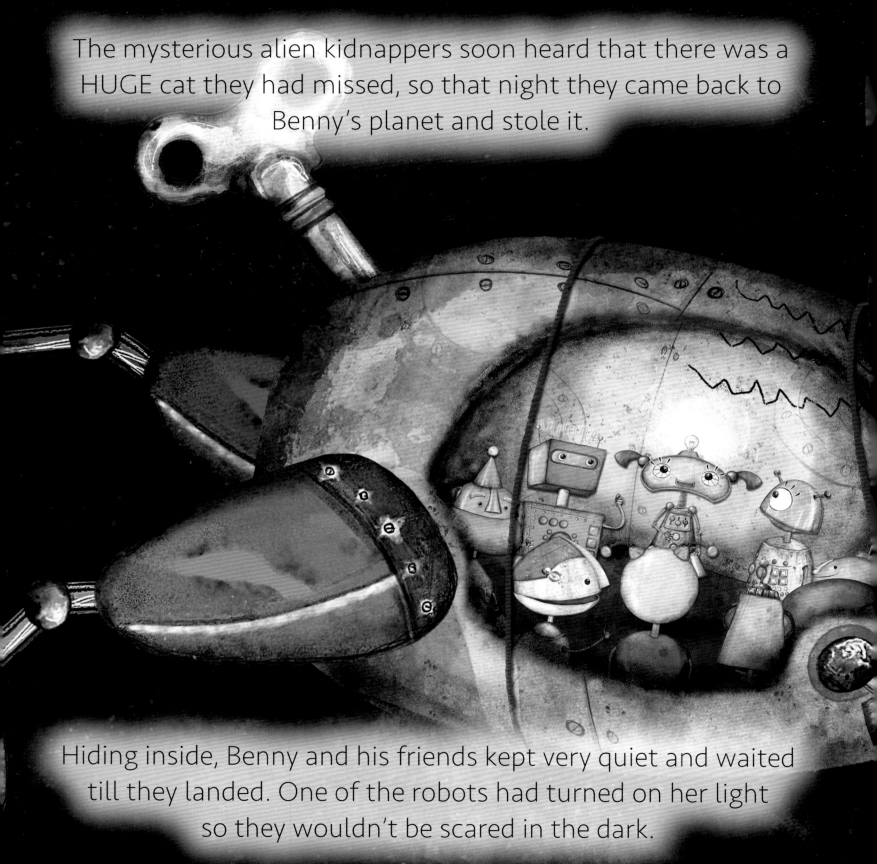

The mysterious alien kidnappers soon heard that there was a HUGE cat they had missed, so that night they came back to Benny's planet and stole it.

Hiding inside, Benny and his friends kept very quiet and waited till they landed. One of the robots had turned on her light so they wouldn't be scared in the dark.

The aliens were really tired
when they got back home
so they all went straight to bed.

Benny quietly opened the secret door and the robots crept out.

It didn't take them long to find all of their missing pets, who were very happy to see them. They were quietly sneaking away...

...when suddenly one of the robots accidently pressed his button and loud, booming music started to play.

The aliens all woke up and started chasing the robots.

The loud music was still booming, making them all wobble so much that they were bouncing off each other and they all fell to the ground.

Benny and his friends stopped running and started helping the wobbly aliens up.

WE ARE REALLY, REALLY SORRY, BUT WE JUST WANTED TO GET OUR PETS BACK.

The Wobblies said they were really, really sorry too, but they had heard the cats were very good at washing dishes and they just needed someone to help them wash theirs.

Just then, Benny remembered there was another page
with the plans he had got when he pressed his big red button.

He looked at the new page, showed it to the Wobblies
and they all started dancing around wobbling, happily,
hugging all the robots.

The new plan showed them
how to recycle the
Wobblies' space ship
and the metal from the
GIGANTIC cat
and make the
BIGGEST dishwasher
they had ever seen.

Everyone worked together and afterwards
they all had some lovely cake and washed their dishes
in the new machine they had all made.

Benny knew exactly what to do.
He told everyone to hold hands and paws together, then, once again,
he placed his finger over his big, bright, red button and pressed it.
There was a…

ZING!

ZANG!

and a very loud…

and everyone went zooming into space,
flying together all the way back home.

They all made it home just in time for the Cool Cats competition which Sparky's friend Sandy won.

THE END.